Big Air!

Extreme Snowboarding and Freestyle Skiing

Phillip Simpson

Contents

Snowboarding and Freestyle Skiing

Winter sports are sports that are played on ice and snow. Traditionally, winter sports were played in winter in places where it snows. Or they were played all year round in places like the **Swiss Alps**, where there is always ice and snow.

There is a huge variety of winter sports, from sledding down a giant snow-covered slope to playing ice hockey on an ice rink, or skiing or snowboarding down a snowy mountain.

A snowboarder competes at the 2010 Vancouver Winter Olympics in Canada.

Snowboarding and **freestyle** skiing are two very popular winter sports. The equipment and skills involved in snowboarding are similar to surfing and skateboarding. A snowboarder uses a board to slide, jump and spin over snow, instead of over water or hard ground. A freestyle skier uses two skis and two ski poles to perform tricks, flips and spins on the snow.

Over time, snowboarding and freestyle skiing have become so popular that some athletes are able to compete in them full-time, as professional athletes.

A freestyle skier competes in the big air event at the 2020 Lausanne Winter Youth Olympics in Switzerland.

Snowboarding

How Snowboarding Started

Snowboarding began in the 1960s in the USA, when surfers and skateboarders started using their balancing, gliding and turning skills on the snow. In 1965, Sherman Poppen, an engineer from Michigan, USA, created the first snowboard by joining two wooden snow skis together and attaching a **rope tether** to the board, so that it could be steered as it glided down a snowy hill. By the 1970s, competitions offering cash prizes for snowboarders were being held.

The first snowboarders were surfers and skateboarders.

Early snowboards were like wooden surfboards for the snow, and they did not have **bindings** for snowboarders to fasten their ski boots to the boards. This meant that the snowboards were hard to control and thought to be dangerous. In fact, snowboarding was considered so unsafe that by the 1980s, snowboarding was banned at most public **ski resorts**. Despite these challenges, the sport continued to grow in popularity.

Early snowboarding was like surfing on the snow.

By the early 1990s, new ski technology and modern materials such as plastic gave snowboarders a much smoother ride. The new materials were stronger and more flexible than wood. The first "high-back" bindings were produced, which enabled snowboarders to lock their boots into place on the board.

Soon, snowboarding was the fastest-growing winter sport in the world, with an estimated six million participants. Ski resort owners, unwilling to miss out on so many paying customers, finally opened their doors to snowboarders.

a ski resort in France

Snowboarders ride the aerial lift to the top of the slope at a ski resort.

Snowboarding at the Olympics

Snowboarding was recognised as an Olympic sport for the first time in 1998, at the Nagano Winter Olympics in Japan.

At these Olympics, there were two snowboarding events. The first event was the giant **slalom**, where competitors raced downhill between a series of obstacles. In the second event, competitors performed acrobatic tricks along a semi-circular ditch covered in ice and snow. This event was called the "halfpipe" because the ditch looked like a large pipe sawn in half.

A snowboarder competes in the halfpipe event at the 1998 Nagano Winter Olympics.

Other snowboarding events were gradually introduced at later Olympics. These included the giant parallel slalom and the snowboard cross. In 2014, the snowboard slopestyle event was added to the Olympics, and in 2018 the big air event was added.

A snowboarder competes in the slopestyle event at the 2014 Sochi Winter Olympics in Russia.

Snowboarding Events

There are a variety of snowboarding events. They test athletes' skills, speed and creativity. In some events, competitors race against other snowboarders, navigating a series of obstacles. In other events, snowboarders compete one by one to try to do the best tricks or make the highest jumps.

Giant Parallel Slalom

In the giant parallel slalom, two snowboarders compete against each other, racing down a mountain on two parallel tracks. Each track has evenly spaced pairs of poles or flags called "gates" for the snowboarder to weave between. The gates are 27 metres apart. Competitors can reach speeds of up to 70 kilometres per hour as they hurtle from gate to gate.

Two snowboarders race on parallel tracks in the giant parallel slalom event.

Parallel slalom

The parallel slalom is very similar to the giant parallel slalom, except the track or course is not as long as the giant slalom course. The gates are closer together – between 8 and 15 metres apart – so the turns made by the athletes are much tighter.

The parallel slalom event requires snowboarders to turn sharply to pass through the gates.

Snowboard Cross

The snowboard cross is a race between four snowboarders down a snow-covered slope. The event was named for its similarities to the sport of motocross, where motorbike riders compete on a course containing many obstacles. In the snowboard cross, competitors must ride their boards as fast as they can through a tight course over jumps and other obstacles and around steep turns.

Four athletes race through a course featuring jumps and other obstacles in the snowboard cross event.

Snowboard Slopestyle

Snowboard slopestyle is an individual event, meaning that the snowboarders do not race against other athletes. Inspired by skateboarding, slopestyle gives athletes a chance to demonstrate their freestyle skills. Snowboarders must navigate a downhill course through jumps, up ramps and along rails. The rails are similar to the handrails that freestyle skateboarders slide along.

Competitors are judged according to how difficult each trick is, the distance and height snowboarders reach in their jumps, the variety of tricks and the athlete's overall performance.

In the slopestyle event, snowboarders perform tricks on rails, ramps and jumps.

Big Air

In the big air event, individual athletes slide down a 21 metre-long snowy ramp that is 13 metres tall. After the snowboarder leaves the ramp, they fly through the air, doing their best tricks – a combination of spins, flips and **grabs** – before landing on snow. Often, they will land as far as 27 metres from the end of the ramp.

Competitors are judged on how difficult their moves are, the variety of their tricks, their "air time" (how long they were in the air) and how good their landing is.

In the big air event, athletes perform snowboard tricks high in the air.

Snowboard Halfpipe

In the snowboard halfpipe event, athletes perform tricks, flips and jumps inside the halfpipe, moving from one side to the other.

The halfpipe event is not a race, so athletes have time to show off their best tricks. Judges give each competitor a score based on how varied and difficult their tricks are, how well they use the halfpipe, the height of their jumps and the overall quality of their performance.

The halfpipe is shaped like a huge snowy pipe that has been cut in half, in which snowboarders perform their tricks.

Freestyle Skiing

How Freestyle Skiing Started

Freestyle skiing began in Europe during the 1930s and 1940s, when skiers began to attempt to do jumps off ramps or ledges or to do other tricks. Freestyle skiing was first known as "stunt skiing" or "acrobatic skiing".

The sport of freestyle skiing became popular in the USA in the 1960s, due partly to advances in ski equipment. During this time, skis became slimmer and the bindings that held skiers' boots in place became stronger. These changes allowed skiers to try more complex tricks.

A Norwegian skier performs freestyle skiing tricks at a winter festival in 1966.

Skiers started to include tricks that were more acrobatic. The sport slowly gained popularity as skiers tried to ride jumps and **moguls** in the most creative ways, aiming for as much air time as possible.

The first freestyle skiing competitions took place in 1971, where competitors were scored based on the reactions of the crowd and who got the loudest cheers. During this time, skiers began attempting bigger jumps and tricks.

US skiers perform freestyle skiing tricks for a photo shoot in 1973.

Freestyle skiing became an official sport in 1979, when rules were introduced into professional competitions. For example, in mogul skiing, the rules require skiers to complete a course without losing control. For aerial contests, where jumps are bigger, rules were introduced to limit the tricks and flips that skiers could attempt, to ensure safety for the competitors.

In the 1990s, some skiers questioned whether such rules were restricting competitors' creativity. This led to the creation of new events, such as the ski halfpipe and the ski slopestyle.

The first acrobatic skiing competitions took place in 1996 in the USA. Inspired by freestyle snowboarding, skiers attempted the same tricks as snowboarders.

A skier competes in the slopestyle event at the Winter X Games in 2004.

Freestyle Skiing at the Olympics

In 1988, freestyle skiing made its first Olympic appearance at the Calgary Winter Olympics in Canada. Moguls became officially accepted as an Olympic sport in 1992, and aerial skiing in 1994. Ski cross, inspired by the similar snowboarding event, first appeared at the 2010 Vancouver Winter Olympics in Canada.

Freestyle skiing now also includes the ski halfpipe and ski slopestyle. These events were added to the 2014 Sochi Winter Olympics in Russia. The freestyle big air event was new to the Olympic program for the 2022 Beijing Winter Olympics in China.

A skier participates in aerial skiing at the 1988 Calgary Winter Olympics.

Freestyle Skiing Events

Freestyle skiing gives skiers an opportunity to express themselves and showcase their skills and tricks in a variety of events. There are six freestyle events in the Winter Olympics: aerials, moguls, ski cross, halfpipe, slopestyle and big air. Each event consists of a skier attempting aerial tricks, flips and spins over jumps, rails or horizontal platforms called "boxes".

Aerials

In the aerials event, athletes ski down a slope one at a time and then jump off a 2- to 4-metre ramp, flipping, twisting and somersaulting as they fly through the air. Competitors are scored according to their skills, the difficulty of their routine and their landing.

In aerial skiing, making a successful landing is as important as pulling off an impressive trick.

Moguls

In the moguls event, individual competitors navigate through a course made up of moguls and jumps. They are judged according to how quickly they complete the course, the difficulty of their jumps and the general skill level displayed.

Jakara Anthony won a gold medal for Australia in the women's moguls at the 2022 Beijing Winter Olympics.

An athlete skis around moguls and over jumps.

Ski Cross

In the ski cross event, athletes compete against three other skiers. The course is made up of big-air jumps and steep turns. Each competitor tries to cross the finish line before the others. If a skier grabs or contacts other competitors in any way, they can be **disqualified**.

Four athletes race against one another in the ski cross event.

Ski Halfpipe

The ski halfpipe is similar to the snowboard halfpipe event. Competitors ski along the halfpipe, displaying their best jumps, flips, spins and somersaults while trying to get as much "air" (or height) as possible. Judges grade their general performance and landings.

Athletes try to get as much air as possible when performing tricks in the ski halfpipe event.

Ski Slopestyle

In this individual event, competitors ski across a course made up of a number of obstacles including rails, boxes and jumps. Each skier is allowed to choose their own route through the course and select which obstacles to attempt or avoid.

The ski slopestyle course includes jumps, boxes and rails.

Freeski Big Air

Freeski Big Air is similar to the big air event in snowboarding. Competitors launch themselves off a large ramp and into the air. During the jump, they complete complex tricks and somersaults and try to finish with a "clean" landing, meaning they land without stumbling, wobbling or falling over.

A skier prepares to kick off from the top of the big air course.

Both snowboarding and freestyle skiing are challenging and difficult sports. Competitors must be highly trained and have nerves of steel. Only the bravest of athletes are able to face hurtling down steep snow-covered slopes and jumping off ramps at great heights, before spinning and tumbling through the air.

To compete in such events, athletes must also be prepared for injuries. One mistake can end in disaster. Only athletes with the strongest will and determination to succeed, combined with rigorous training, can take a medal in the Winter Olympic Games.

Interview with New Zealand Freestyle Skiing Champion

Nico Porteous

Olympic Gold Medallist, Men's Halfpipe

In 2018, at the PyeongChang Winter Olympics in South Korea, 16-year-old Nico Porteous made history as New Zealand's youngest-ever Olympic Games medallist when he won a bronze medal in freestyle skiing (also called freeskiing) halfpipe. It was New Zealand's third-ever Winter Olympic medal. At the 2022 Beijing Winter Olympics, Nico became New Zealand's second Winter Olympic gold medallist when he won the men's halfpipe.

Nico Porteous with his Olympic gold medal in 2022

Nico Porteous as a boy

How did you get into skiing?

I got into skiing when I was growing up, through my mum and dad. They were very keen skiers when they were younger. The first time I skied was on a family holiday in France where the whole family could ski, apart from me. I was the one sitting at home with Mum while [my brother] Miguel and Dad went skiing. So, Mum taught me how to ski, and I've just progressed from there.

Tell us a little about your training schedule and diet.

My weekly training schedule normally involves four to five days on snow, one or two trampoline sessions where I work on air awareness and new tricks, and three gym sessions where I work on strength and landing patterns for injury prevention.

My diet is well balanced. I make sure I always have a good breakfast with protein and carbohydrates (for example, chicken and rice) before a big day skiing. I always take snacks onto the mountain so I have access to nutrition while I am skiing, to increase the length of time that I can train for.

If I have a day off, one of my favourite foods to eat is a big juicy cheeseburger!

What is your favourite event and why?

My favourite event is the X Games, held in Aspen, USA, because of the freeskiing history that has been created there. X Games is the foundation of freeskiing. There have been so many world firsts and important moments that have happened at X Games. We compete at night under floodlights with the crowds watching on from below – it creates an awesome atmosphere and Aspen is a really special place.

What is your favourite sporting moment?

This is a tough one. There are two moments that stand out in my mind. The first is the 2022 Aspen X Games where I landed the best run of my life under huge pressure. The second moment is the Beijing 2022 Olympic Winter Games. To be able to achieve my lifelong dream of winning an Olympic gold medal for New Zealand is indescribable.

Nico Porteous at the 2021 X Games in Aspen

What was it like to win a gold medal?

To win a gold medal was the biggest relief I have had in my life. It just felt like this tonne of bricks had been lifted off my shoulders. I had put so much pressure on myself to perform in that moment – I have been dreaming of it since I was a little kid, it was just so special. It can be hard to find words to describe the feeling.

What challenges did you come across in getting where you are today?

In sport, you come across challenges every single day. One of the big ones for me is the amount of time I spend away from home and on the road. I am lucky to get to see so many amazing places, but it is a challenge living out of a suitcase at times. Overcoming injury is another huge challenge – you need to remain really disciplined and focused to recover from an injury.

Nico Porteous training in New Zealand in 2021

What are your strengths as both an athlete and a person?

I think my strengths as an athlete are the ability to identify the things I am good at and then utilise them to my advantage. I have become really good at switching off in really stressful moments, turning off my brain and trusting my body to do the work. Personally, I always strive to be true to myself and be the best person that I can be.

What advice would you give to young people wanting to compete in freeskiing events?

Dream big, work hard and be yourself, don't try and be someone you're not.

Nico Porteous competing in the halfpipe event at the 2022 Beijing Winter Olympics

Glossary

bindings (*noun*) straps and clips that hold an athlete's foot in place on a snowboard or ski

disqualified (*verb*) excluded from continuing in the competition

freestyle (*adjective*) when any style can be used in a sport

grabs (*noun*) moves where a snowboarder reaches down and grabs the edge of their snowboard in mid-air

moguls (*noun*) large bumps or mounds of snow

rope tether (*noun*) a rope attached to early snowboards, used to control them

ski resorts (*noun*) places people stay to ski, snowboard and do other winter sports

slalom (*noun*) a ski race along a winding course marked by poles

Swiss Alps (*proper noun*) a mountain range in Switzerland that is famous for its snow-covered slopes

Index